# There's a Spaceship in the Hot Tub!

By

## Marg McKinley

Illustrated by Cheryl A Cadzow

Printed in Australia

Published by Author Academy Elite
PO Box 43, Powell, OH 43035
www.AuthorAcademyElite.com



Identifiers:
LCCN: 2020919662
ISBN: 978-1-64746-554-4 (paperback)
ISBN: 978-1-64746-555-1 (hardback)
ISBN: 978-1-64746-556-8 (ebook)

Available in paperback, hardback, e-book, and audiobook

*Book design by Jetlaunch. Cover design by Jetlaunch.*

# TABLE OF CONTENTS

# CHAPTER 1
## THE HOT TUB!

Millie burst into the room. She slammed the door hard against the wall. "There's a spaceship in the hot tub!" she cried out.

Ben rolled over from his bed where he lay on his stomach, watching YouTube videos on his iPhone.

"Millie, what are you talking about?" he said. He yawned and stretched his arms in the air.

She rushed over to her brother's bed and sat down excitedly. "I was just out there. There's a spaceship in the hot tub!" She grabbed Ben by the arm and pulled him towards the door.

Ben rolled his eyes and smiled. He was protective of his little sister, but was she exaggerating again? At only six years old, she had a rather vivid imagination. He stood up and followed Millie down the passage and opened the back door. The wooden building that contained the hot tub was a long way down the back yard, set in the corner with a beautiful view of the rolling green fields outstretched behind it. As they hurried down the yard with Millie pulling at Ben's arm, the sun beat down on their backs. It was the start of summer in Australia, and the sun's rays burnt through Ben's t-shirt.

Ben and Millie came to the door of the little wooden room. Millie put her finger to her lips. "Shhhh. Don't scare them away."

Ben slowly opened the door. Inside, the hum of the spa pump and smell of the moisture in the hot air surrounded them.

They walked cautiously across to the hot tub. Millie quietly peered over the edge into the water. It was still there! She pointed at it without making a sound.

"Look," she whispered, "there it is, there it is!"

Ben looked over the edge of the hot tub, and a small floating object bobbed on the surface of the water. It was rounded like a spaceship and had a small door at the base of it.

He opened his mouth, but Millie stopped him suddenly. The small door began to slide open. Ben quickly pulled Millie down out of view as the door slid back, and a long arm-like device slowly extended outward. It appeared to be some kind of platform. Holy moly! It had two little men standing on it—tinier than action figures out of a cereal box. They started to chat incessantly.

"Darce, you really should be more careful. Someone could've seen us," one of the little men said.

"Sorry, Tom. It looks like we're in the clear, though," Darce said.

They climbed into a little round device attached to the end of the platform and sped off to the edge. Millie and Ben stayed out of sight, trying not to breathe too heavily for fear of being heard. Tom threw a rope over the edge of the hot tub, and it hooked firmly over the side. He then climbed the rope up onto the edge of the hot tub. He was so tiny. It was crazy! It was like someone had put him into a shrinking machine, and voila—a tiny person appeared. He wore a green t-shirt and blue shorts. A black baseball cap held down his curly red hair. Darce pulled himself up onto the edge as well. He was as small, maybe smaller, and wore a brown t-shirt with black shorts and a black cap.

As the little men headed out of the crack in the door, Millie sneezed. The little men froze. Ben slapped his hand across her mouth. She let out a scream, and the little men looked directly at them.

It's ok," Ben said. "We will not hurt you." He slowly got up, holding his hand out towards them. "We won't hurt you. Who are you? And what are you doing here?" he asked.

The little men looked at each other in shock. Nervously shaking from head to toe, Tom replied, "We are from Gazlay, a planet far away."

Millie stood up, holding tight onto Ben's arm.

"Gazlay," Ben said. "Where is that?" This was all a bit weird for Ben. First, they met these tiny people, and then they said they were from another planet. They looked normal enough. But in all the movies, people from outer space have two heads or space suits that all look the same. He wondered what Gazlay looked like. Was it like Earth?

"It's on the other side of the universe," Tom said.

"Wow!" Millie said in awe. Tom looked at Millie and smiled.

"We are not here to hurt you, either," he said. "We have been shrunk down to midgets so we can travel through outer space in our little spaceship."

"Just a minute," Tom said. He turned to Darce, and before their eyes, Tom and Darce transformed into normal-sized people, like popcorn in a popping cup.

*What the …* Ben thought. He looked at Millie, who looked as shocked as he was. They weren't men at all! They were about the same age as Millie and Ben.

Ben gulped hard. "You had better sit down and tell us what's going on." He led them to a table with four chairs where his parents often sat for a coffee or a cold glass of orange juice. His hand shook as he pulled out a chair. *Another planet,* he thought. *What could this mean?*

# CHAPTER 2
## NEW FRIENDS

Tom and Darce sat down, followed by Ben and Millie. "It's like this," Tom said. He began to tell them all about Gazlay, a planet where people had fun. "We fly in outer space in our space jets and have races. One day, I went so fast to beat my friend I couldn't see anything. I nearly crashed into another planet. It was so funny." Tom stood up; a big smile lit up his face. He held his arms up like he was holding a steering wheel. "We fly around in loops and dodge and weave to miss each other." He turned sharply in his imaginary space jet. "It's so much fun!" He laughed.

Ben and Millie looked at each other.

"Tell us more," Millie said.

Tom went on. "On Gazlay, though, technology has become so advanced we no longer have trees or plants. Not even animals—our pets are robots. Our main focus in life is to simply have fun, but it's become dull. Nothing is real anymore. Our trees and flowers are wall murals, and our robot pets don't have personalities. That is why we have travelled so far. We want to discover how people on other planets live and what they do to have fun."

"Interesting," Ben said.

Tom stood up from his seat and extended his hand to Ben. Ben was pleased. He shook Tom's hand with a warm smile.

"You should've seen us on the spaceship," Darce said. "It was so much fun! We zoomed at the speed of light." He shot his arm across the sky. "We shot past stars and Jupiter. It was awesome!"

Tom smiled as he sat down. "Alright, Darce." He could only imagine how shocked Ben and Millie would be if they had not transformed themselves into Earthlings.

Ben and Millie looked on intently as Tom went on.

"On Gazlay, we focus on the good things in life. Whatever we do, we have fun. Our elders have sent us to Australia as our first mission—to learn how you have fun. You do have fun, don't you?" Tom asked with a grin.

Millie shouted out, "I know how to have fun!" She leapt out of her seat, shooting her hand up in the air like she was in school. She jumped up and down, eager to start having fun with her new friends.

"Great," Tom said. He stood up ready for action, excited by Millie's enthusiasm. "Where shall we begin?"

"Hang on!" Darce said. "We were not supposed to be seen by Australians."

"It's ok, Darce—I will sort that out later."

Ben was a bit confused. This idea of simply having fun …
*What sort of a world do they come from?* Usually, he got into
trouble if he had too much fun. Just last week at school, he
and his mates made sling shots from sticks they found in the
yard and rubber bands they had left over from science class.
They found all these really cool rocks and were shooting each
other on the butt. It stung like crazy, but it was so much fun
until the teacher came along and gave them detention for
dangerous behaviour. They were only having fun.

Tom looked at Ben. "It's like this," he said. "On Gazlay,
you do what you love and love what you do. Only then will
all the rewards in life come to you."

"That sounds cool," Millie said excitably. "Come on, Ben—
we know how to have fun!"

Tom and Darce smiled at the excitement in Millie's eyes.

"Where will we start?" Tom asked as he glanced towards Ben.

"Hmmm," Ben said, "it's fun in the hayshed."

"Ok, let's go," Darce said as he jumped out of his seat.
He was eager for fun!

Ben and Millie lived on a farm where there were lots of
fun things to do. Ben led the way as they all headed off to
the hayshed.

# Chapter 3
## The Secret Tunnel

Millie skipped excitedly behind Ben. Her little skirt flounced around her thin legs. Ben swept his thick dark hair across his forehead and opened the big squeaky wooden door to the hayshed.

"Wow! That's a lot of hay!" Tom said.

"Follow me." Ben jumped onto the second rung of bales. "This is the tunnel to our secret hideout." He squeezed himself between two small bales of hay.

Millie crawled in behind him and waved their new friends in. "Come on. It's fun."

Tom and Darce looked at each other, smiled, and climbed in. As Tom twisted and turned up the narrow tunnel, straw poked into his side. It pierced his skin. Blood dripped from the deep scratch in his leg, and it stung ferociously. There was no air, and his chest felt tight. It was difficult to breathe. A glimpse of light shone through the gaps between the bales, and he could just make out the direction of the tunnel. He kept moving forward, winding through the small space. *How long will this take?* he thought. *This is no fun!*

"I'm out," Ben said. He squirmed to the top and wiped the loose straw from his t-shirt. Millie crawled out, followed by Darce, and then Tom.

"At last," Tom said as he gasped for air. He climbed out of the tunnel, opened his mouth to complain, but his jaw dropped in awe. The radiant sun shone through an old glassless window. The rainbow-coloured glow lit up the whole area in an indescribable kaleidoscope of colour. "This is spectacular!" He stood there amazed. He had never seen anything like this on Gazlay.

They sat down on the make-shift chairs built from hay bales. Ben pulled out a model aeroplane.

"What's that?" Darce asked.

"It's an aeroplane," Ben said. "One day, when I'm a pilot, I'm going to soar through the air in an aeroplane, just like this one." He handed it to Darce.

"Cool! It's like a spaceship." Darce examined the model aeroplane and wondered how different it really was than his spaceship.

"Not quite," Ben said. "It's not as fast."

Darce swooped the aeroplane through the air. Millie began to tell Tom and Darce all about farm life and the animals and how they built the tunnel. The sun shifted from the window. Tom caught a glimpse of the rolling hills across the paddocks, stretched to the edge of where land meets sky. The huge gum trees blew gently in the wind. The cows in the paddock were black and white dots, heads down, feeding on the lush green grass. He lay near the window with his face propped in his hands and dreamed a little. *This place is magic*, he thought.

Suddenly, Darce stood up. "What is that?" he said, holding his hand in the air. Yellow goo dripped from his fingers. "Oh, gross!" He turned around. Yellow goo was stuck to the back of his shorts. "This stuff stinks!" He tried to brush it off.

"Ha, ha," Millie laughed. "You've sat on a rotten egg."

Ben reached behind the bale he was sitting on and pulled out another egg. "I have a whole basket of eggs down the bottom." He had a wicked grin on his face. "Who wants to have a rotten egg fight? You want to have fun? Let's go!" He leapt over the edge.

Tom and Darce were amazed. They looked over the edge as Ben landed way down below on his back, cushioned by the soft loose hay.

Millie jumped behind him. "Come on," she cried.

"How cool," Tom said. He glanced at Darce. They both laughed, leapt over the side, and landed on the heavenly bed-like hay.

The luxurious feeling was brought to an abrupt end. Ben grabbed an egg and took aim at Tom. He hit him on the arm. "Gotcha!" Tom looked around. Ben laughed. The goo rolled down into his palm. He ran to the basket, grabbed a couple of eggs, and threw one at Ben. Ben ran from the shed. His heart pumped wildly with excitement.

Millie picked up an egg, and Darce started to run. She hit him in the middle of his back. "The greener the egg, the rottener it is!" she yelled.

He turned to Millie. "You won't get away with that!" Millie shrieked and ran outside.

They all burst from the hay shed, goo dripping from their clothes. The stench was rife. They dodged and weaved to miss the eggs. Exhausted, they rolled onto the soft green grass covered in rotten stinking egg.

"That was fun!" Tom puffed.

Just then, Mum appeared around the corner, hands on her hips. "What is going on here?"

"Oh no," Millie said, "we've been sprung … Mum, we were only having fun."

Mum went off her tree. She yelled and ranted on and on. Darce and Tom were taken by surprise. What happened? They were having fun. Why was this mum lady so angry?

"But, Mum, we met some little people and had so much fun with them."

"Millie, stop telling fibs and come in and get yourself cleaned up," she said sternly. She was too angry to even notice Tom and Darce. Millie dragged her tired little body across the yard to the house. Her hair was a tangled mess, and a mixture of green and golden yolk dripped from her curls. Ben smiled through the egg yolk that covered half his face. It wasn't worth trying to explain to Mum; she wouldn't believe them anyway. *Adults are no fun!*

Darce and Tom were a little confused as they made their way back to their spaceship in the hot tub.

"I wonder what she will do to them?" Darce said.

"Not sure. On Gazlay, you would be rewarded for such fun. It didn't look like Ben and Millie were going to be rewarded. They were lucky to have this lush green grass, haystacks, and rotten eggs. It was so much fun. This mum lady should lighten up and enjoy herself more."

As he walked along, Tom thought about the narrow tunnel with no air and how uncomfortable he felt. He decided it really was worth a little bit of pain to experience such fun and beauty. The magic of the rainbow sun would be etched into his memory forever. He looked forward to tomorrow—Ben and Millie knew how to have fun.

# CHAPTER 4
## A WILD RIDE

Early the next day, Millie ran into Ben's room. She was more excited than ever. "Let's see if Tom and Darce are still here."

"Definitely!" They hurried down the path. Ben pulled the door back to see Tom and Darce sitting at the table.

"We are glad to see you guys," Tom said with a smile. "Are you up for more fun today?"

Ben looked at Tom with a devilish smile. "I have planned a fun ride."

"Great," Tom said. His eyes lit up.

"Right," Ben said. "Millie, go and get the keys to the old ute. We are going to take these boys for the ride of their life." Millie bounced with joy. She loved having fun with her big brother. It was her most favourite thing to do.

When she returned, the boys had collected buckets of dried cow dung.

"Alright," Ben said. "We need teams of two. Millie, you go with Tom … Darce can come with me. You can drive, can't you, Tom?"

"Yeah, sure, Ben. I'll give it a shot." *How hard could it be?* he thought.

"Right!" Ben said. "Drive the ute across the paddock with the windows down. Slowly, ok?"

Millie was excited. Tom slipped into the driver's seat and started the motor. *Good,* he thought, *pretty much the same as vehicles on Gazlay.* Millie scrambled in beside him. They headed across the paddock, wound down the windows, and slowly drove back.

As they approached, Ben hurled a cow pat through the window. It smashed into the side of Tom's face. He laughed out loud. "You guys are crazy!" he yelled out the window.

Millie giggled, holding her hand cheekily across her mouth. "That looked funny."

A cow pat smacked into the side of her head and splattered across her face. "I think that one was still a bit damp." She pulled the crumbled bits from her curls. Another cow pat tumbled off the side of the window and down the front of her dress. She giggled. Darce kept throwing the cow pats at her. All she could see was dung as it flew through the air.

Ben put up his arm as a signal to stop. He walked over to Tom with a big smile. "Having fun?"

"You betcha!" Tom threw back his head with a loud laugh.

"Come on, then. It's your turn to toss the cow poo at us," Ben said. Tom and Millie climbed out of the ute. They dusted off the crumbled cow pats.

Ben and Darce drove like crazy. The old ute battled to keep up with the sharp turns. Ben turned the wheel hard and ducked to avoid the flying poo. Darce bounced across the seat like a bouncy ball. A cow pat smashed into his face. He laughed out loud.

They were covered in crumbly cow pat pieces. No amount of dodging and swerving could beat the right arm curve of Tom. He was well known for his bowling arm on Gazlay. Ben ducked to miss a flying poo, but when he lifted his head, he was hit right between the eyes. He could not see. His foot slammed onto the accelerator. The ute hit top speed as it flew across the paddock. Ben hit the brakes hard. The wheels squealed as the ute turned sharply and sped towards a huge gum tree. He swerved at the last second, and the ute slammed into the fence. The front of the ute was smashed. Smoke billowed out from the raised hood. Millie screamed and ran towards them. Tom followed.

She ran to Ben. "Are you ok?" she asked. Ben and Darce climbed out of the ute.

Ben looked at Darce, concerned for his new friend. "I'm ok. What about you, Darce?"

"Yeah, I'm ok," he said.

Millie hugged her brother. Then, she hugged Darce.

"Uh, oh …" Ben said. "Here comes Dad." They could see the dust fly across the paddock as the ute quickly approached.

Dad screamed to a halt and sprung out of the ute. He glared at Ben. "What the hell is going on here?"

"Sorry, Dad," Ben said. He hung his head low.

"I've a good mind not to let you kids go to the footy this afternoon. Are you alright? Who are these kids?"

"This is Tom and Darce—they are new kids at school," Ben said. "I can do chores later to make up for it. Please, let me go to the footy."

Over the initial shock, Dad realised they were not hurt and calmed down. He looked at Tom and Darce. "Nice to meet you boys," he said.

There was a long pause as Dad thought for a moment. "Ah … I was young once, I suppose. Alright, I will worry about the ute later."

"Awesome! Thanks, Dad." Ben grinned. "Can Tom and Darce come too?"

"Who do you barrack for, boys?"

"Hawthorn," Ben chimed in quickly. These Gazlians would not know what Australian rules football was.

"As long as you barrack for the mighty Hawks, consider yourselves invited, boys. One condition—we keep the whole ute thing from your mother. No use upsetting her today."

"What ute?" Ben said cheekily.

"That's the spirit, son." He winked and patted Ben on the head.

Millie hugged her dad. "You are the best, Dad."

"Come on, then. Let's get you kids cleaned up. The footy starts in just over an hour." They jumped in the back of the ute and headed off to get ready for the footy.

*This dad guy is pretty cool,* Tom thought.

"You guys are going to love the footy," Ben said. He smiled to himself. *These Gazlians will never be the same after they watch a game of Australian rules football.*

# CHAPTER 5
## A TRIP TO THE FOOTY (AUSTRALIAN STYLE)

"What's footy?" Tom asked.

Ben slipped a brown and gold Hawks footy jumper over his head. "Australian rules football. It is the best sport in Australia. You'll love it! There's a practice match down at Marong. Hawthorn v Collingwood. It's not often the big guns come to the country." He passed Hawks footy jumpers to Tom and Darce. "Here, put these on."

It was a different sort of fun, but Tom and Darce needed to experience it—especially the crazy Pies supporters. Ben grinned to himself.

"Come on! In the car, kids!" Dad called. "We don't want to miss the start."

They arrived at the ground. It was a warm day. The Marong Footy Oval was set in the bush surrounded by huge gum trees.

The grass on the oval was freshly mowed and ready for action. There were cars crammed along the fence. The fans were pumped. The game was about to start.

Hawthorn (the mighty Hawks) ran onto the field as the siren sounded. The Hawks supporters dressed in brown and gold cheered for them.

"That's my boys," Ben yelled. He puffed out his chest like they were his personal friends.

"Go, Hawks!" Millie yelled.

Tom and Darce grinned. The noise was crazy loud.

"This is awesome," Tom yelled. Ben grinned widely. The crowd let out another roar. Collingwood (the Pies) ran onto the field. They bounced balls and sprinted across the oval in zig zags, keen to begin. The noise was exhilarating! The crowd roared with enthusiasm. A small town like Marong hadn't seen this sort of action before.

A Pies supporter dressed in black and white waved a large sign that said *Go Pies!* She screamed wildly; "Come on, Pies!"

Ben looked at Tom. "What do you think?"

"The crowd is pretty crazy!" He wasn't sure what was going to happen. Guys in green shirts and grey shorts appeared. They had whistles and flags. One of them held a football above his head.

"They're the umpires," Ben said.

Tom nodded. Darce stood wide-eyed, amazed at all the people. They waved streamers and flags. Brown and gold. Black and white. One of the umpires held the football high in the air. The siren sounded. He blew his whistle and bounced the ball. The game was on! People cheered. Tom and Darce looked stunned.

A group of people yelled at the umpires. "That was a free!"

Ben glanced at Tom and Darce and began to laugh. A Hawks player grabbed a Pies player and flattened him onto the ground. The umpire blew his whistle loudly and gestured towards the Hawks player. "Free kick to Hawks."

"You useless umpires!" a Pies supporter yelled. She waved her fist. "Did you get your certificate out of a cereal box?"

Ben laughed. Tom was dumb-founded by this wild lady. *What is she on?* he thought. The game was close. The Hawks broke away in the third quarter to a three-goal lead. Ben was excited. "Up the mighty Hawks!" he yelled, pumping his fist.

The siren sounded. The Hawks had a three-goal lead with one quarter to play. Who was going to win from here?

Out came the players for the final quarter. A Pies player took a flying leap in the air. He climbed high onto the back of a Hawks player and took a screamer of a mark, right in front of the goal. He walked towards the goal. Ball out in front. He kicked the ball high, and the crowd watched on as it soared between the big sticks. It was a goal! The Pies supporters all rose, arms raised. They chanted the Pies theme song, "Good old Collingwood forever." The atmosphere was contagious.

Tom yelled, "Go Hawks!" and waved his fist in the air.

Ben gave him the thumbs up. "Two minutes left on the clock," he yelled.

The Pies got another goal. The Hawks now led by one goal. The ball bounced into the Hawks' forward, but they were unable to goal. The Hawks player grabbed a Pies player and slammed his face into the grass. The whistle sounded! "Free kick to Collingwood," the umpire shouted. The Pies supporters cheered.

The Pies passed the ball on quickly from one player to the next. The Hawks desperately tried to stop them. A Pies player swiftly led in front of the pack and took a mark. Ten seconds left on the clock. Would he kick a goal? Would the scores be level? If he missed, they would lose.

He walked back to take his kick, turned, and faced the goal posts. He took a deep breath. Could he do it? The Pies fans clung to hope.

The Pies player approached the goal and kicked a wobbler high in the air. A breathless crowd waited in suspense. The ball was suspended in the air as it soared across the sky, and at the last minute, it veered off to the left and nicked the post. It was a point. Hawks won!

The Hawks' supporters jumped for joy. The Pies' supporters yelled abuse at the umpires, but it was no use. The game was over. The Hawks players piled on top of each other as their theme song echoed across the ground. "We're a happy team at Hawthorn …" The players gave the crowd high fives as they exited the arena.

Tom drew a deep breath. "Wow, what can I say?"

"That was awesome!" Darce said.

"You bet," Millie said. "Hawks win!" She pumped her fist in the air.

As they drove back home, Tom wondered how he was going to explain this event to the elders on Gazlay.

"That was great," Ben said. "How about we go for a swim when we get home?"

Millie looked up wide-eyed at Ben. "Can we go to Diamond Hill?"

Ben looked at Millie with a smile. "My plan exactly. Let's take the dogs. Besides, you can't come to Australia and not experience the great Australian bush."

# CHAPTER 6

## HIDDEN DANGERS IN THE BUSH

Ben and Millie had two dogs. Max was a cheeky brown and white Jack Russell, and Jedda was an energetic red Kelpie.

"Come on, boys," Millie called to the dogs. They ran to her, and she hugged them both. "Good dogs."

Off to Diamond Hill they headed. They walked across the last paddock and met the edge of the bush. Ben stopped.

"Wow," Darce said. "That's a lot of gum trees." He looked high above. The glorious gum leaves glinted in the sun as they swayed gently in the soft warm breeze.

"Be careful where you step," Ben said. "Brown snakes slither along the ground. They can kill you if you get bitten." Darce looked worried. He wasn't sure he wanted to look and feel like an Earthling right now. "Don't worry. We'll be alright," Ben said. "The dogs will scare them away,"

They headed into the bush. The dogs jumped with enthusiasm. *Real dogs are so happy,* Tom thought. *Such simple lives. Nothing upsets them. Ben yelled at them, and then they licked his face like it didn't happen. They must have superpowers to be so happy all the time.*

They pushed aside small bushes and branches that blocked the path. Suddenly, Darce screamed. He had a terrified look on his face.

"What is it?" Tom said.

"It's a snake." He shook all over. They looked down at his foot.

Ben laughed. "That's a branch off the gum tree. If it was a snake, it would've bitten you and slithered away by now." They all laughed. Darce breathed a sigh of relief.

They climbed higher and higher up the hill. "The view is magnificent," Tom said. He looked down across the tops of the thick gum trees. Extreme satisfaction spread across his face.

"It's not far now," Ben said.

They arrived at a small dam. Bulrushes lined the far side of the water's edge. The dam was peaceful. The water, like glass. So still you could see your reflection in it. Tom looked up at a branch that hung over the dam. It had a long rope with a stick tied to the end.

"That's a swing rope," Ben said. "Come on! Let's give it a shot."

"I'm in," Tom said and jumped up eagerly.

Ben grabbed the rope. He swung himself far out across the water, let go, and hurled himself into the middle of the dam. A massive splash of water billowed up behind him.

"That's wild!" Tom cried out. He grabbed the rope and swung hard out into the water, let go, and landed splat in the middle of the dam. "That's crazy, wild fun," he yelled.

Ben dragged himself from the water and sat on the edge. Tom duck-dived deep into the water and then popped up to the surface. He lay on his back for a moment as he enjoyed the serenity of the cool flowing water. All of a sudden, he screamed. "Help!" He slapped at his stomach. He grabbed at his legs. "I've been bitten. Are they little snakes? They won't come off!" The colour ran from his face.

Ben held out his arm towards him. "Come on, Tom! They are leeches. You are not going to die."

"They will suck all your blood out," Millie said cheekily.

Tom swam erratically towards the shore. The pain of these sucking creatures brought tears to his eyes.

"They're not snakes," Ben repeated. "They are leeches. They won't hurt you."

Tom jumped out of the water. He hit at the leeches as they sucked his blood. Finally, the last leech was freed, and he began to relax.

"Leeches!" Ben said. "They are annoying, but they won't kill you. That makes for a short swim, though. It's not so pleasant when the little suckers latch on."

They sprawled out on the water's edge to relax. The water was once again peaceful and calm.

Tom started to laugh. "I must've looked funny."

"Yeah ... well," Ben said, "what can I say? You were slashing about like a crazy man."

They all laughed. Ben thought it was pretty cool how these new friends always saw the funny side in everything. It made life so much simpler, easier, and more fun.

Millie stood up. She picked up a small, flat rock. "Darce, look at this. When you can't swim near water, you can skim rocks." Darce liked the way Millie always thought of something fun to do. He stood up and followed Millie to the water's edge.

Millie bent down and flicked her little rock across the top of the water. It bounced four skips. Max jumped in the water after it. He ducked his head to grab the rock. Jedda leapt across the dam towards Max. He loved the water.

"That looks like fun!" Darce searched on the water's edge for a flat rock. He bent down and tossed the rock across the water. Plop! He was disappointed.

"That's ok," Millie said. "Give it a little flick." She demonstrated the swing of the wrist. Darce found another flatter, smoother rock. He skimmed it beautifully four skips across the top of the water.

"Wow," he said, "that feels great!"

"That's it," Millie said. "You did it perfectly."

He stood up with a huge grin on his face and began to search for another flat rock, eager to repeat the performance.

"Well," Ben said as he stood up, "we'd better head home." They gathered the gear and started the long arduous trek down the hill. Just as they came clear of the bush, Tom received a message. He took a small device out of his pocket that had buzzed.

"It's the elders. I wonder what they want." Tom put his hand on Darce's shoulder with a look of concern on his face. "Come on, Darce. Let's get back to the spaceship and find out."

They took off back to the spaceship. Millie looked up at Ben. "I hope they don't have to go home."

# CHAPTER 7
## BLAST OFF

Ben opened the door and scanned the room. Where were Tom and Darce?

Millie pointed into the hot tub. "The spaceship is still there. Look, here they come." The little boat sped to the edge. Ben was relieved. Moments later, they popped into life-sized people.

"We are to prepare to leave," Tom said.

"Oh no!" Millie said. "When?"

"The elders have advised we must head back today."

Darce nodded. He was excited to go home but sad to leave. He'd had so much fun. It was great they had met Ben and Millie who knew how to have fun.

"Do you think you will come back?" Millie asked.

Ben looked anxiously at Tom.

He put his hand on Ben's shoulder. "I'm not sure."

"Come on." Millie pulled them in. "Group hug." They all hugged for a final good-bye.

"Well, Darce, it's time to go." Tom and Darce stepped aside and, with a zap of light, were tiny figurines once again.

Millie could see Darce's tiny hand wave from the spaceship as the door closed. *So cute,* she thought.

***

Inside the spaceship, Tom and Darce prepared for take-off.

"That was so cool," Darce said. "It would be great if we could come back again."

"It certainly would, Darce!"

They buckled their seat belts and guided the spaceship out of the hot tub, through the door, and into the sky.

Millie ran outside. She waved frantically. Ben ran behind her. With a flash, the spaceship shot into outer space.

"Well, that's it," Ben said. They turned to walk towards the house.

Millie slipped her little hand into Ben's as they walked. She felt so happy to have met these new friends and a little sad they were gone.

Ben looked at Millie with a smile. He wondered if they would ever return.

***

"Well, Darce," Tom said, "that was an excellent take-off."

"Do we have to delete their memories?"

"Yes, Darce, we do."

***

With a flash of light, Ben sat bolt upright and opened his eyes. His mum knelt over him and Millie. "What's going on?" he said. Millie drowsily began to wake.

"Ben, Millie, are you ok?" Mum said. Tears welled in her eyes.

"Ah … yeah," Ben said. He looked around, confused.

"You've both been unconscious. Did you hit your heads?" she cried. "I've been so worried!"

"It's ok, Mum. Chill out—we're ok," Ben said. *Was it all just a dream?* he thought. He looked at Millie. She looked back with a look of knowing in her eyes.

It appeared to their mother they had been unconscious. He knew that somehow something real had happened.

***

As the spaceship zoomed through outer space, Tom smiled at Darce. "They had seen us, but I didn't erase all of their memories."

Darce was pleased. He smiled and put his hand on Tom's shoulder. "We will come back, won't we, Tom?"

"I reckon it'd be a good thing to do, Darce." With wide smiles, they sped towards Gazlay. Will they be back? For now, no one knows.

# ABOUT MARG MCKINLEY

Marg grew up on a farm in Victoria, Australia. Her background is in teaching, and she is now a grandmother of two. The fun memories Marg has of her childhood, as well as her love of children and country living, created this book.

Marg always finds the joy in life. She wrote this book to instil fun and adventure into the minds of her readers.

Her love of writing and telling stories has always inspired her!

You can connect with Marg at her website: marg-mckinley.com.

# ABOUT CHERYL A CADZOW

Cheryl has drawn all her life and dabbled in painting. She has been a potter, photographer, country reporter, and video editor. She now focuses on writing and illustration.

In 2008, Cheryl was introduced to digital art and has not stopped. She has been part of the Hitrecord Community since 2013. Hitrecord has won two Emmys of which she was one of the artists involved with animation art. Cheryl lives in Victoria, Australia.

Cheryl A Cadzow
instagram.com/cheryl_a_cadzow/

www.ingramcontent.com/pod-product-compliance
Lightning Source LLC
Chambersburg PA
CBHW051747050726
47598CB00003B/1366